Mary, Mary

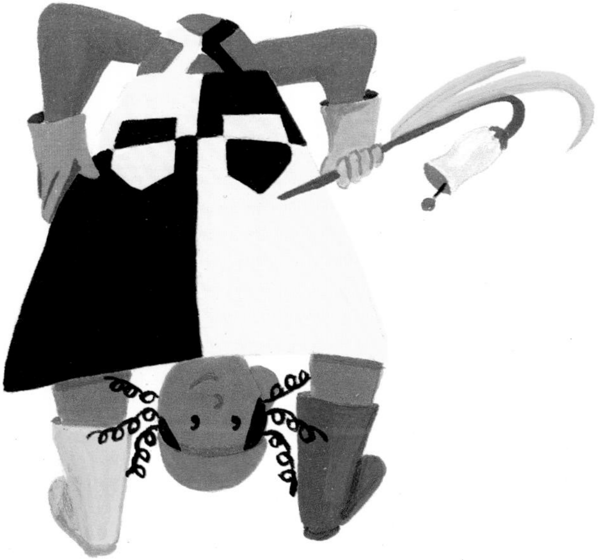

Illustrated by Jane Burns

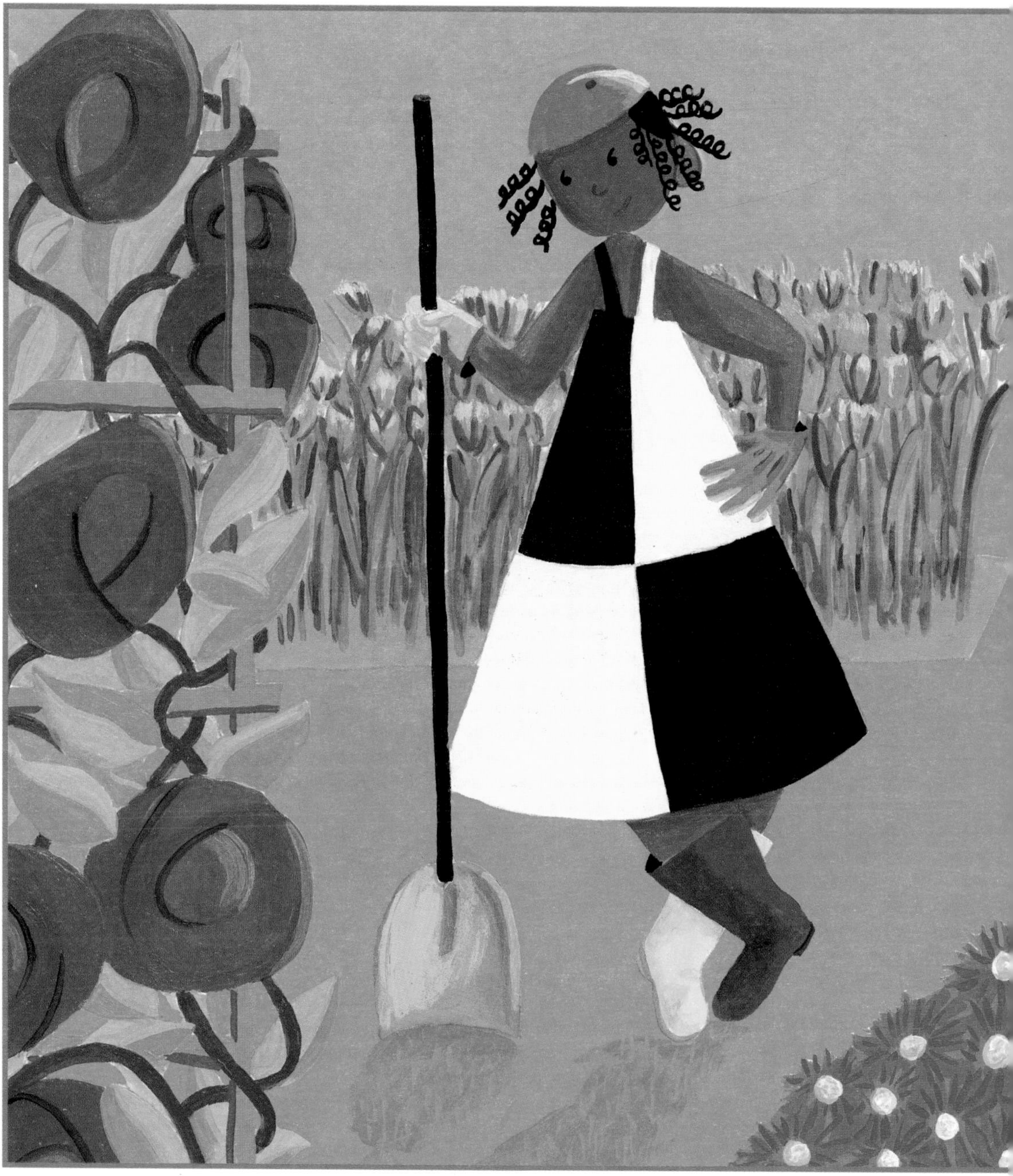

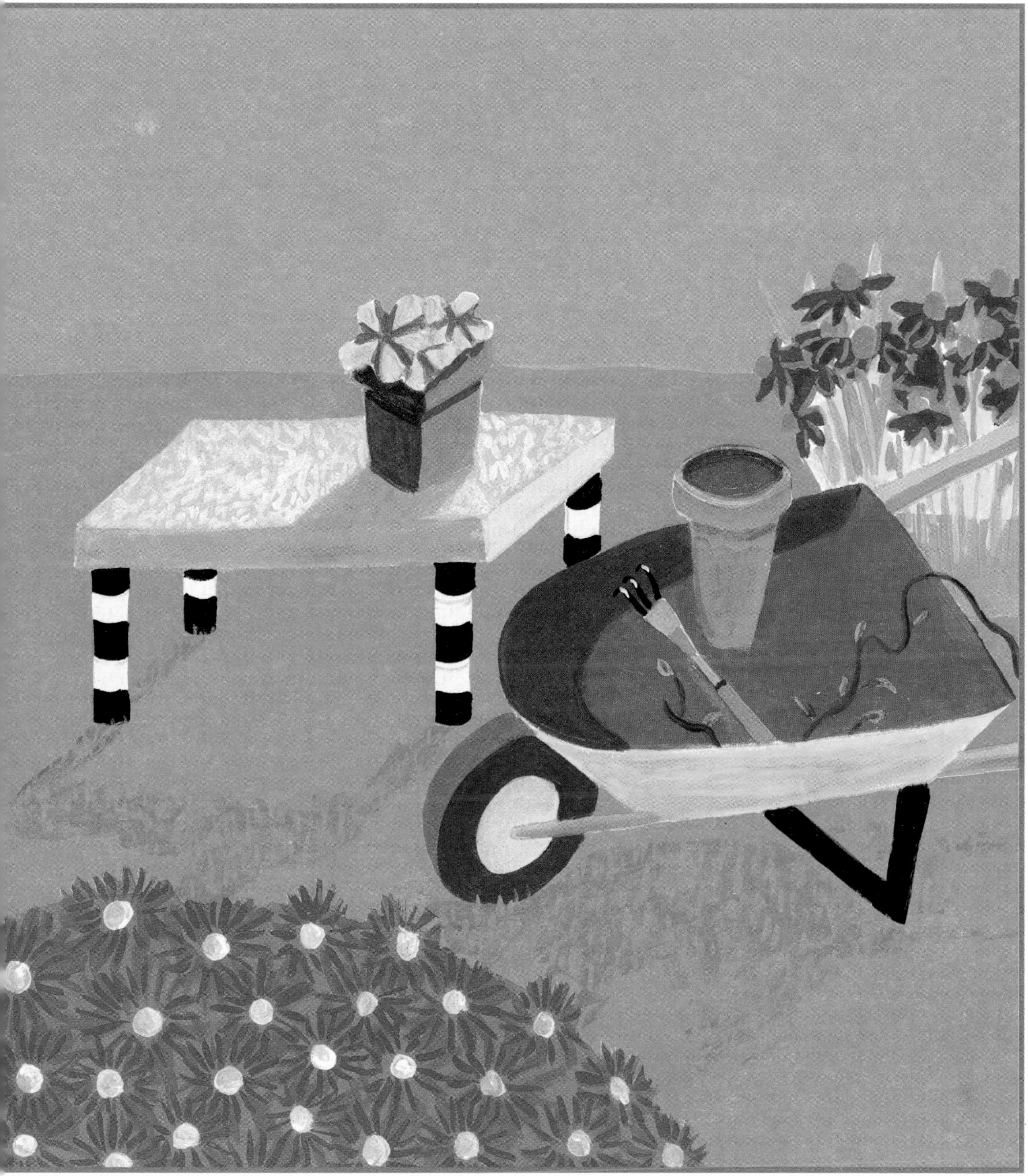

Mary, Mary quite contrary

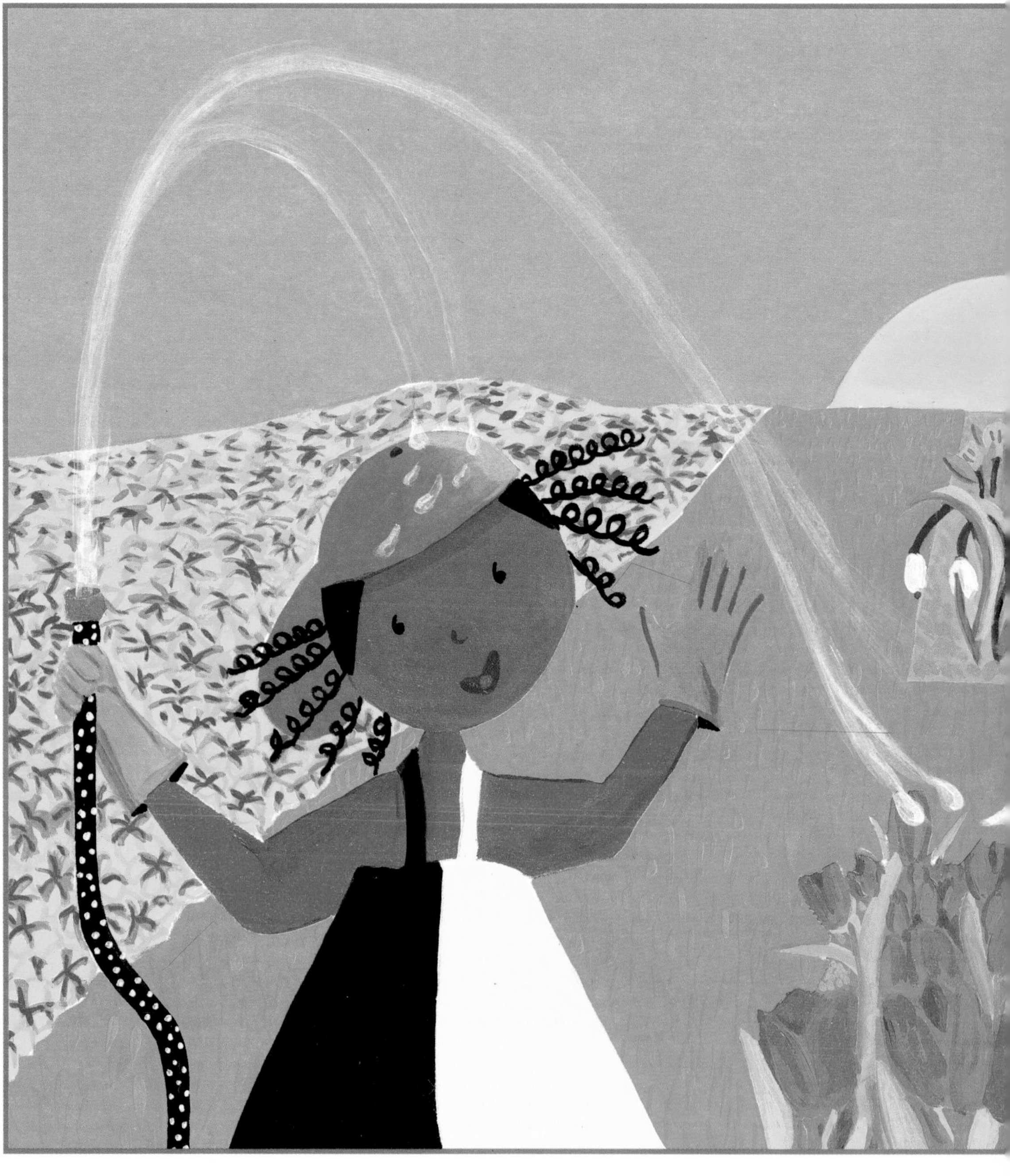

How does your garden grow?

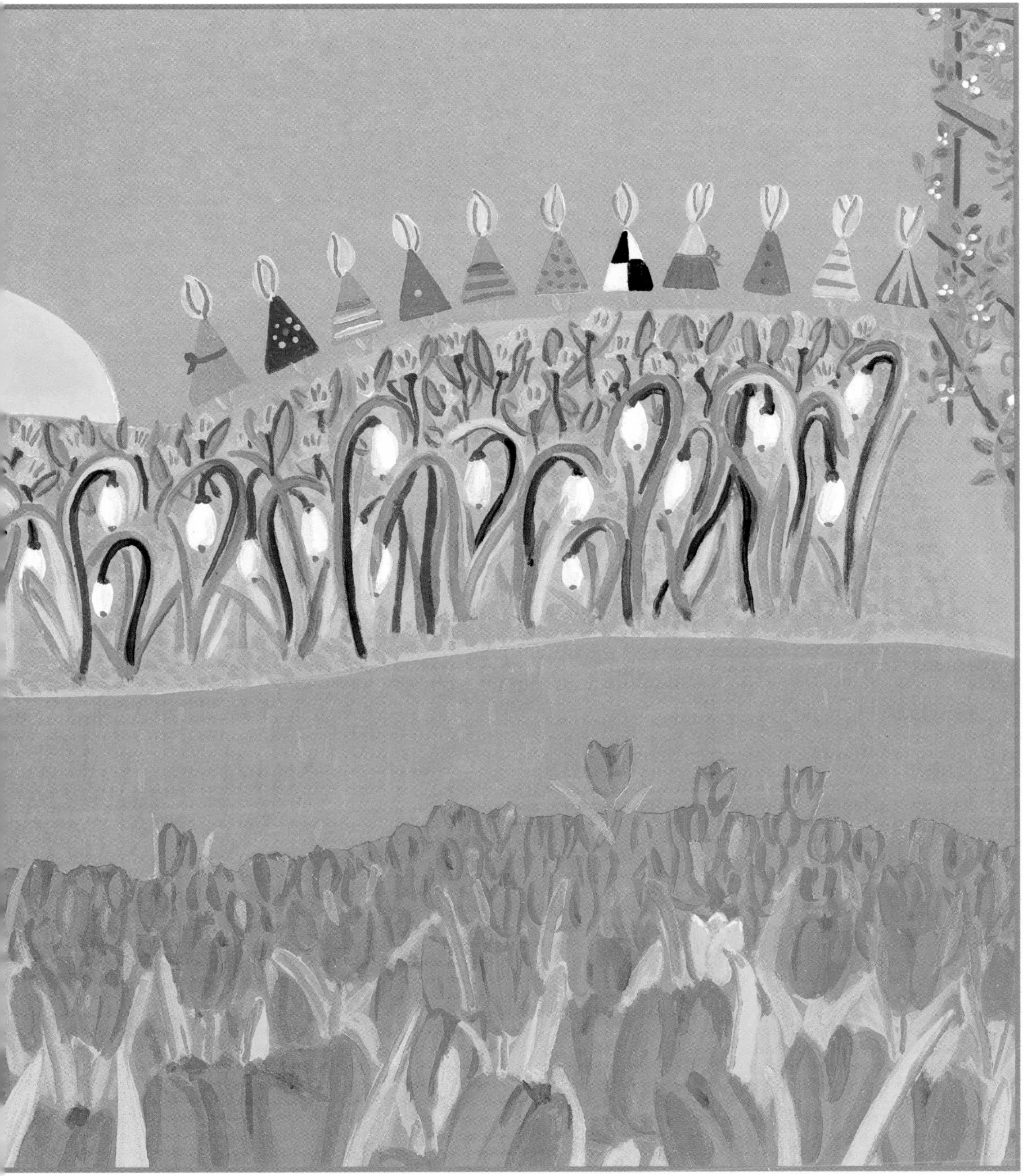

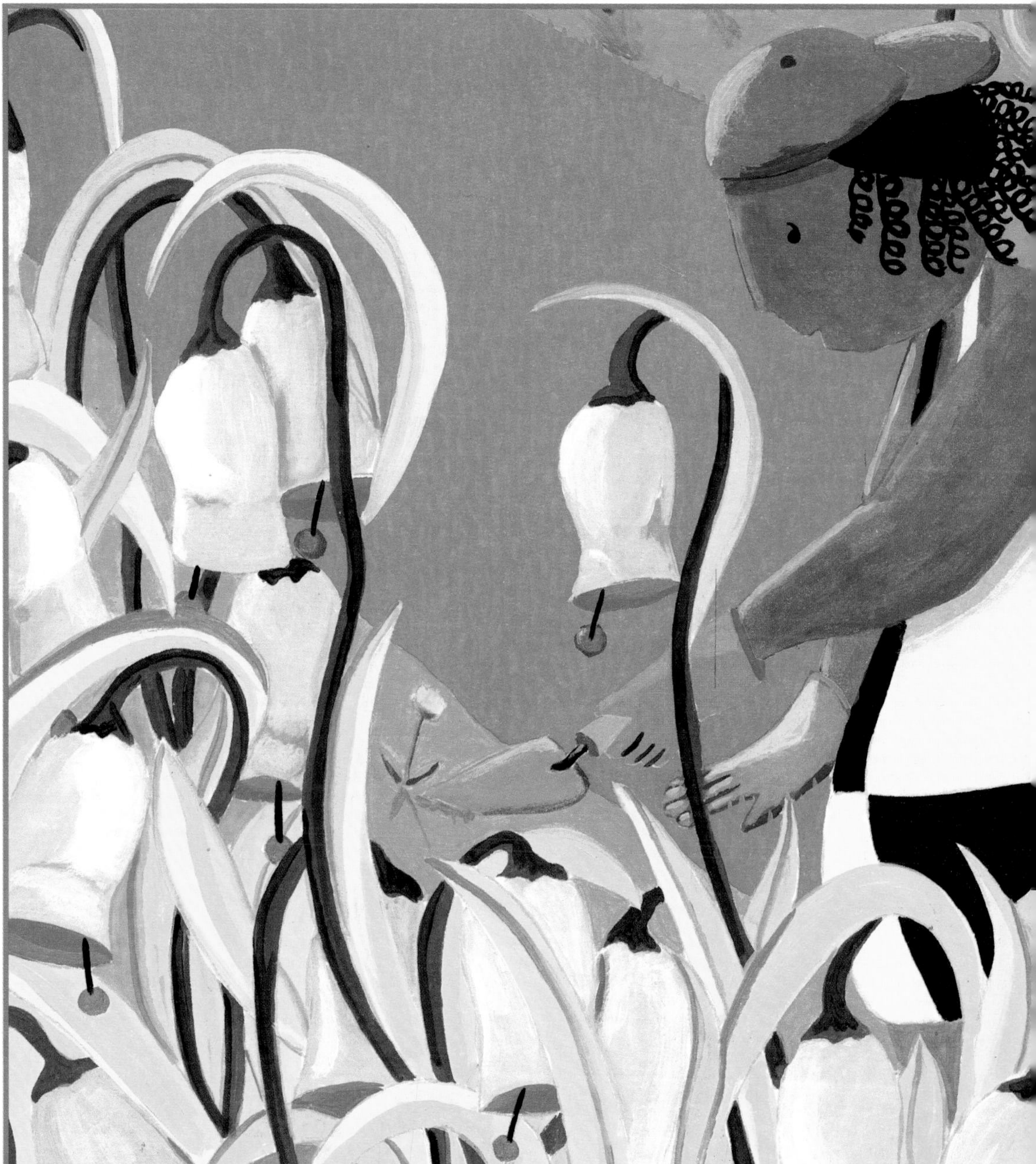

With silver bells,

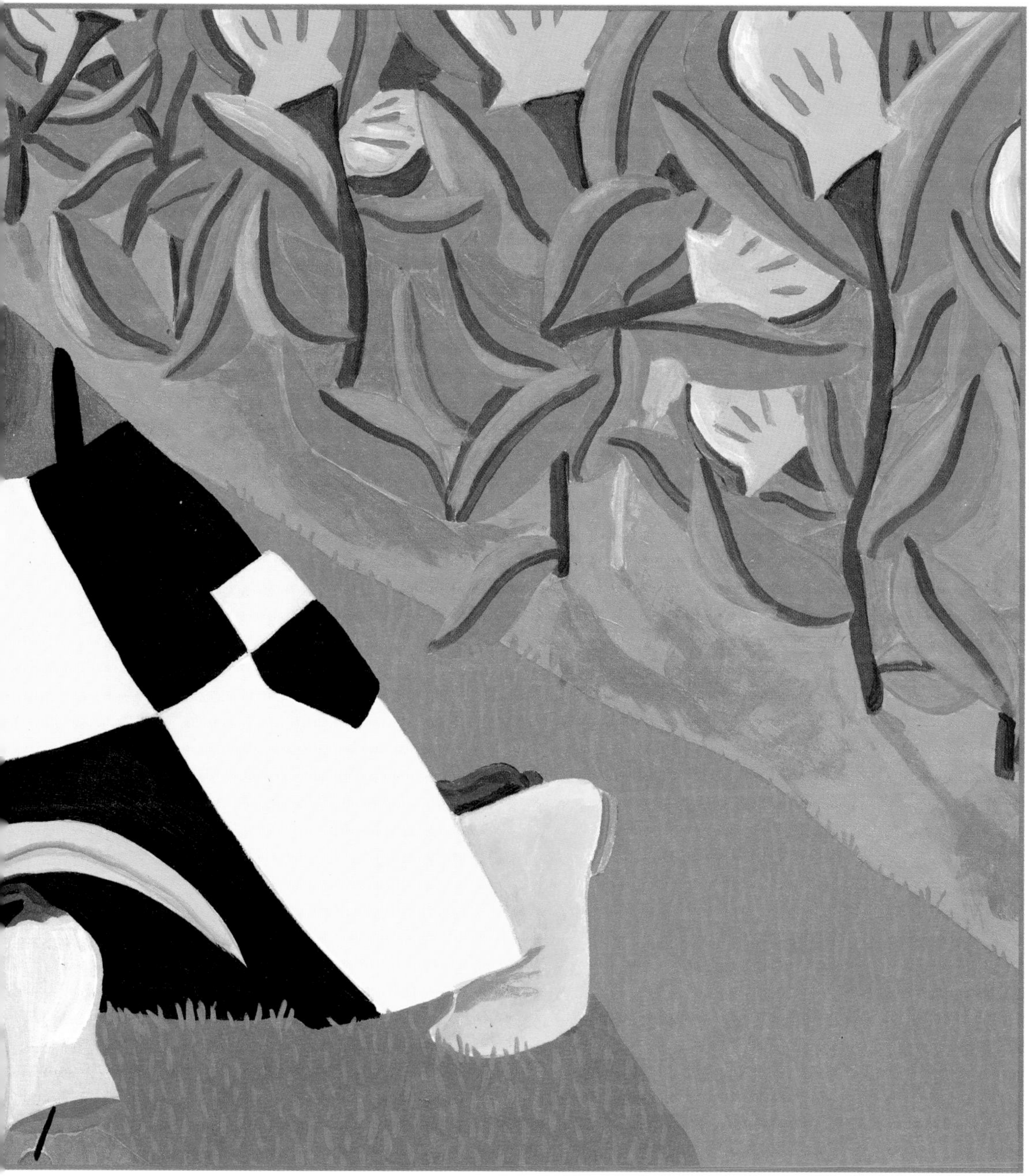

And cockleshells,

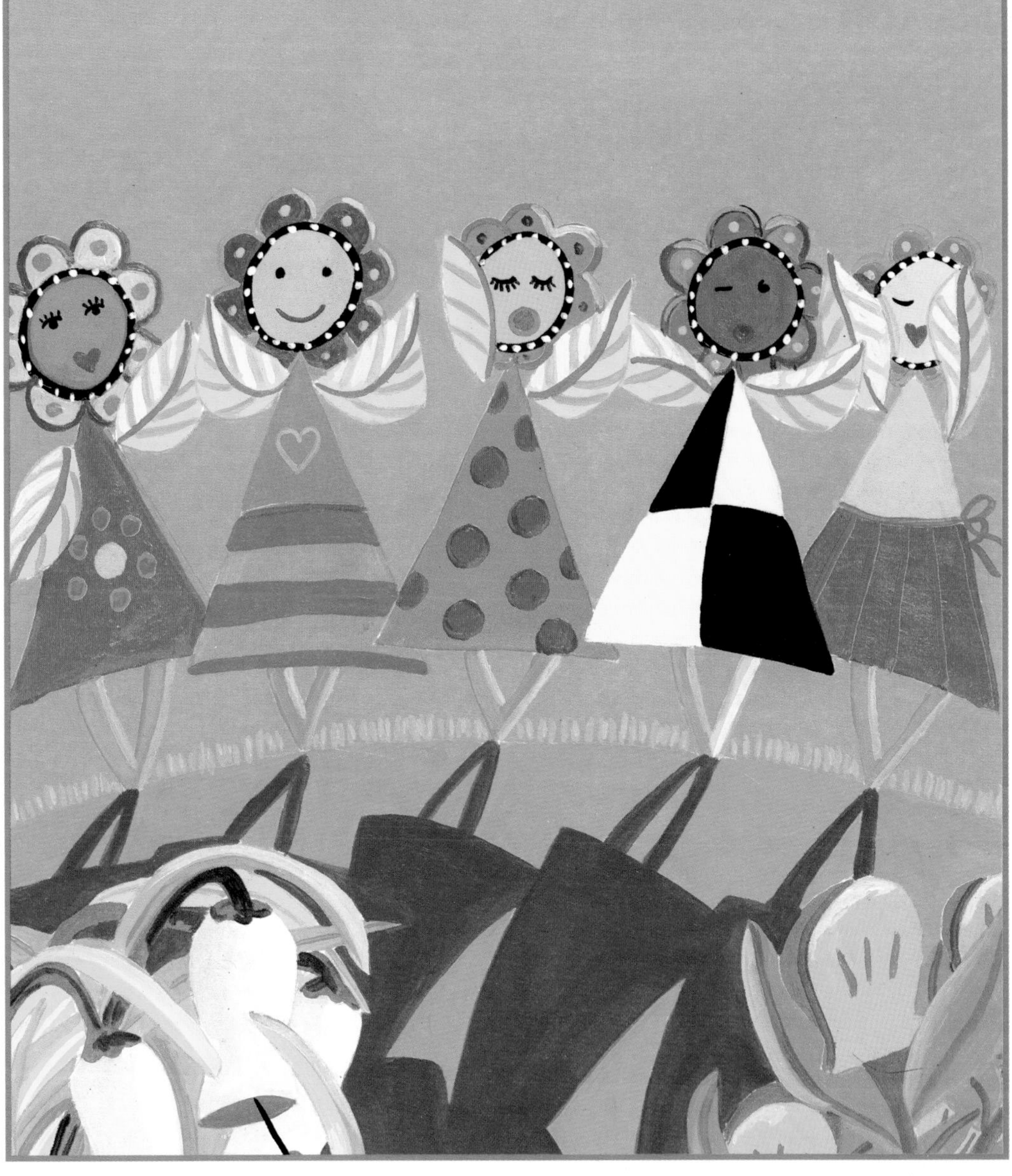

And pretty maids all in a row.